The Cat's Meow

Warren Kimble

Walker & Company ❋ New York

Mat cat

Clean cat

Fluffy cat

Scaredy cat

Curious cat

Playful cat

Fat cat

Twin cats

Proud cat

Happy cat

For Christopher Warren Kimble, who loved cats. —W.K.

First published in the United States of America in 2006 by
Walker Publishing Company, Inc.
Distributed to the trade by Holtzbrinck Publishers

For information about permission to reproduce selections from this book, write to Permissions, Walker & Company,
104 Fifth Avenue, New York, New York 10011.

Library of Congress Cataloging-in-Publication Data
Kimble, Warren.
  The cat's meow / Warren Kimble.
    p. cm.
  ISBN-10: 0-8027-8078-4 [hardcover]
  ISBN-13: 978-0-8027-8078-2 [hardcover]
  ISBN-10: 0-8027-8079-2 [reinforced]
  ISBN-13: 978-0-8027-8079-9 [reinforced]
  1. Kimble, Warren—Juvenile literature. 2. Cats in art—Juvenile literature. I. Title.
  ND237.K52A4 2006   2005043465

The illustrations for this book were created using acrylic Winsor & Newton paint on distressed wood.

Book design by Nicole Gastonguay

Visit Walker & Company's Web site at www.walkeryoungreaders.com

Printed in China

10 9 8 7 6 5 4 3 2 1